'We were sitting on the porch, tutti-frutti melting on our plates, when suddenly, just as we were wishing that something would happen, something did; for out of the red road dust appeared Miss Bobbit'

TRUMAN CAPOTE
Born 30 September 1924, New Orleans
Died 25 August 1984, Los Angeles

'Children on Their Birthdays' and 'A Tree of Night' were first published in book form in *A Tree of Night and Other Stories*, New York, 1949. 'A Christmas Memory' was first published in book form as a stand-alone hardback edition, New York, 1966.

ALSO PUBLISHED BY PENGUIN BOOKS
Other Voices, Other Rooms · *Summer Crossing* · *Breakfast at Tiffany's* · *In Cold Blood* · *Music For Chameleons* · *Answered Prayers* · *A Capote Reader* · *The Complete Stories*

TRUMAN CAPOTE

Children on Their Birthdays

PENGUIN BOOKS

PENGUIN CLASSICS

Published by the Penguin Group
Penguin Books Ltd, 80 Strand, London WC2R ORL, England
Penguin Group (USA) Inc., 375 Hudson Street, New York, New York 10014, USA
Penguin Group (Canada), 90 Eglinton Avenue East, Suite 700, Toronto, Ontario,
Canada M4P 2Y3 (a division of Pearson Penguin Canada Inc.)
Penguin Ireland, 25 St Stephen's Green, Dublin 2, Ireland (a division of Penguin Books Ltd)
Penguin Group (Australia), 250 Camberwell Road, Camberwell, Victoria 3124, Australia
(a division of Pearson Australia Group Pty Ltd)
Penguin Books India Pvt Ltd, 11 Community Centre, Panchsheel Park,
New Delhi – 110 017, India
Penguin Group (NZ), 67 Apollo Drive, Rosedale, North Shore 0632, New Zealand
(a division of Pearson New Zealand Ltd)
Penguin Books (South Africa) (Pty) Ltd, 24 Sturdee Avenue, Rosebank, Johannesburg 2196,
South Africa

Penguin Books Ltd, Registered Offices: 80 Strand, London WC2R ORL, England

www.penguin.com

Selected from *The Complete Stories*, published in Penguin Classics 2005
This edition published in Penguin Classics 2011
1

'Children on Their Birthdays' copyright © Truman Capote, 1948, 1976
'A Christmas Memory' copyright © Truman Capote, 1956, 1984
'A Tree of Night' copyright © Truman Capote, 1945, 1973

Typeset by Jouve (UK), Milton Keynes
Printed in England by Clays Ltd, St Ives plc

ISBN: 978–0–141–19586–5

www.greenpenguin.co.uk

Penguin Books is committed to a sustainable future
for our business, our readers and our planet.
The book in your hands is made from paper
certified by the Forest Stewardship Council.

Contents

Children on Their Birthdays

This story is for Andrew Lyndon.

Yesterday afternoon the six-o'clock bus ran over Miss Bobbit. I'm not sure what there is to be said about it; after all, she was only ten years old, still I know no one of us in this town will forget her. For one thing, nothing she ever did was ordinary, not from the first time that we saw her, and that was a year ago. Miss Bobbit and her mother, they arrived on that same six-o'clock bus, the one that comes through from Mobile. It happened to be my cousin Billy Bob's birthday, and so most of the children in town were here at our house. We were sprawled on the front porch having tutti-frutti and devil cake when the bus stormed around Deadman's Curve. It was the summer that never rained; rusted dryness coated everything; sometimes when a car passed on the road, raised dust would hang in the still air an hour or more. Aunt El said if they didn't pave the highway soon she was going to move down to the seacoast; but she'd said that for such a long time. Anway, we were sitting on the porch, tutti-frutti melting on our plates, when suddenly, just as we were wishing that something would happen, something did; for out of the red road dust appeared Miss Bobbit. A wiry little girl in a starched, lemon-colored party dress, she sassed along with a grown-up mince, one hand on her hip, the other supporting a spinsterish umbrella. Her mother, lugging two cardboard valises and a wind-up victrola, trailed in the background. She was a gaunt shaggy woman with silent eyes and a hungry smile.

All the children on the porch had grown so still that when a cone of wasps started humming the girls did not set up their usual holler. Their attention was too fixed upon the approach of Miss Bobbit and her mother, who had by now reached the gate. 'Begging your pardon,' called Miss Bobbit in a voice that was at once silky and childlike, like a pretty piece of ribbon, and immaculately exact, like a movie star or a schoolmarm, 'but might we speak with the grown-up persons of the house?' This, of course, meant Aunt El; and, at least to some degree, myself. But Billy Bob and all the other boys, no one of whom was over thirteen, followed down to the gate after us. From their faces you would have thought they'd never seen a girl before. Certainly not like Miss Bobbit. As Aunt El said, whoever heard tell of a child wearing makeup? Tangee gave her lips an orange glow, her hair, rather like a costume wig, was a mass of rosy curls, and her eyes had a knowing, penciled tilt; even so, she had a skinny dignity, she was a lady, and, what is more, she looked you in the eye with manlike directness. 'I'm Miss Lily Jane Bobbit, Miss Bobbit from Memphis, Tennessee,' she said solemnly. The boys looked down at their toes, and, on the porch, Cora McCall, who Billy Bob was courting at the time, led the girls into a fanfare of giggles. '*Country* children,' said Miss Bobbit with an understanding smile, and gave her parasol a saucy whirl. 'My mother,' and this homely woman allowed an abrupt nod to acknowledge herself, 'my mother and I have taken rooms here. Would you be so kind as to point out the house? It belongs to a Mrs Sawyer.' Why, sure, said Aunt El, that's Mrs Sawyer's, right there across the street. The only boarding house around here, it is an old tall dark place with about two dozen lightning rods scattered on the roof: Mrs Sawyer is scared to death in a thunderstorm.

Coloring like an apple, Billy Bob said, please ma'am, it being such a hot day and all, wouldn't they rest a spell and have some tutti-frutti? and Aunt El said yes, by all means, but Miss Bobbit shook her head. 'Very fattening, tutti-frutti; but *merci* you kindly,' and they started

3

across the road, the mother half-dragging her parcels in the dust. Then, and with an earnest expression, Miss Bobbit turned back; the sunflower yellow of her eyes darkened, and she rolled them slightly sideways, as if trying to remember a poem. 'My mother has a disorder of the tongue, so it is necessary that I speak for her,' she announced rapidly and heaved a sigh. 'My mother is a very fine seamstress; she has made dresses for the society of many cities and towns, including Memphis and Tallahassee. No doubt you have noticed and admired the dress I am wearing. Every stitch of it was hand-sewn by my mother. My mother can copy any pattern, and just recently she won a twenty-five-dollar prize from the *Ladies' Home Journal*. My mother can also crochet, knit and embroider. If you want any kind of sewing done, please come to my mother. Please advise your friends and family. Thank you.' And then, with a rustle and a swish, she was gone.

Cora McCall and the girls pulled their hair-ribbons nervously, suspiciously, and looked very put out and prune-faced. I'm *Miss* Bobbit, said Cora, twisting her face into an evil imitation, and I'm Princess Elizabeth, that's who I am, ha, ha, ha. Furthermore, said Cora, that dress was just as tacky as could be; personally, Cora said, all my clothes come from Atlanta; plus a pair of shoes from New York, which is not even to mention my silver turquoise ring all the way from Mexico City, Mexico. Aunt El said they ought not to behave that way about a fellow child, a stranger in the town, but the girls went on like a huddle of witches, and certain boys, the sillier ones that liked to be with the girls, joined in and said things that made Aunt El go red and declare she was going to send them all home and tell their daddies, to boot. But before she could carry forward this threat Miss Bobbit herself intervened by traipsing across the Sawyer porch, costumed in a new and startling manner.

The older boys, like Billy Bob and Preacher Star, who had sat quiet while the girls razzed Miss Bobbit, and who had watched the house into which she'd disappeared with misty, ambitious faces, they now straightened up and ambled down to the gate. Cora McCall sniffed and poked out her lower lip, but the rest of us went and sat on the steps. Miss Bobbit paid us no mind whatever. The Sawyer yard is dark with mulberry trees and it is planted with grass and sweet shrub. Sometimes after a rain you can smell the sweet shrub all the way into our house; and in the center of this yard there is a sundial which Mrs Sawyer installed in 1912 as a memorial to her Boston bull, Sunny, who died after having lapped up a bucket of paint. Miss Bobbit pranced into the yard toting the victrola, which she put on the sundial; she wound it up, and started a record playing, and it played the

5

'Court of Luxemborg'. By now it was almost nightfall, a firefly hour, blue as milkglass; and birds like arrows swooped together and swept into the folds of trees. Before storms, leaves and flowers appear to burn with a private light, color, and Miss Bobbit, got up in a little white skirt like a powderpuff and with strips of gold-glittering tinsel ribboning her hair, seemed, set against the darkening all around, to contain this illuminated quality. She held her arms arched over her head, her hands lily-limp, and stood straight up on the tips of her toes. She stood that way for a good long while, and Aunt El said it was right smart of her. Then she began to waltz around and around, and around and around she went until Aunt El said, why, she was plain dizzy from the sight. She stopped only when it was time to rewind the victrola; and when the moon came rolling down the ridge, and the last supper bell had sounded, and all the children had gone home, and the night iris was beginning to bloom, Miss Bobbit was still there in the dark turning like a top.

We did not see her again for some time. Preacher Star came every morning to our house and stayed straight through to supper. Preacher is a rail-thin boy with a butchy shock of red hair; he has eleven brothers and sisters, and even they are afraid of him, for he has a terrible temper, and is famous in these parts for his

green-eyed meanness: last fourth of July he whipped
Ollie Overton so bad that Ollie's family had to send him
to the hospital in Pensacola; and there was another time
he bit off half a mule's ear, chewed it and spit it on the
ground. Before Billy Bob got his growth, Preacher played
the devil with him, too. He used to drop cockleburrs
down his collar, and rub pepper in his eyes, and tear up
his homework. But now they are the biggest friends in
town: talk alike, walk alike; and occasionally they dis-
appear together for whole days, Lord knows where to.
But during these days when Miss Bobbit did not appear
they stayed close to the house. They would stand around
in the yard trying to sling-shot sparrows off telephone
poles; or sometimes Billy Bob would play his ukulele,
and they would sing so loud Uncle Billy Bob, who is
Judge for this county, claimed he could hear them all the
way to the courthouse: *send me a letter, send it by mail,
send it in care of the Birmingham jail.* Miss Bobbit did not
hear them; at least she never poked her head out the
door. Then one day Mrs Sawyer, coming over to borrow a cup of sugar, rattled on a good deal about her new
boarders. You know, she said, squinting her chicken-
bright eyes, the husband was a crook, uh huh, the child
told me herself. Hasn't an ounce of shame, not a mite.
Said her daddy was the dearest daddy and the sweetest
singing man in the whole of Tennessee . . . And I said,

honey, where is he? and just as off-hand as you please she says, Oh, he's in the penitentiary and we don't hear from him no more. Say, now, does that make your blood run cold? Uh huh, and I been thinking, her mama, I been thinking she's some kinda foreigner: never says a word, and sometimes it looks like she don't understand what nobody says to her. And you know, they eat everything *raw*. *Raw* eggs, *raw* turnips, carrots – no meat whatsoever. For reasons of health, the child says, but ho! she's been straight out on the bed running a fever since last Tuesday.

That same afternoon Aunt El went out to water her roses, only to discover them gone. These were special roses, ones she'd planned to send to the flower show in Mobile, and so naturally she got a little hysterical. She rang up the Sheriff, and said, listen here, Sheriff, you come over here right fast. I mean somebody's got off with all my Lady Anne's that I've devoted myself to heart and soul since early spring. When the Sheriff's car pulled up outside our house, all the neighbors along the street came out on their porches, and Mrs Sawyer, layers of cold cream whitening her face, trotted across the road. Oh shoot, she said, very disappointed to find no one had been murdered, oh shoot, she said, nobody's stole them roses. Your Billy Bob brought them roses over and left them for little Bobbit. Aunt El did not say one word. She just marched over to the peach tree, and cut herself a switch. Ohhh, Billy Bob, she stalked along the street calling his name, and then she found him down at Speedy's garage where he and Preacher were watching Speedy take a motor apart. She simply lifted him by the hair and, switching blueblazes, towed him home. But she couldn't make him say he was sorry and she couldn't make him cry. And when she was finished with him he ran into the backyard and climbed high into the tower of a pecan tree and swore he wasn't ever going to come down. Then his daddy stood at the window and called to him: Son, we aren't mad with you, so come down and eat your supper. But Billy Bob wouldn't budge. Aunt El went and leaned against the tree. She spoke in a voice soft as the gathering light. I'm sorry, son, she said, I didn't mean whipping you so hard like that. I've fixed a nice supper, son, potato salad and boiled ham and deviled eggs. Go away, said Billy Bob, I don't want no supper, and I hate you like all-fire. His daddy said he ought not to talk like that to his mother, and she began to cry. She stood there under the tree and cried, raising the hem of her skirt to dab at her eyes. I don't hate you, son . . . If I didn't love you I wouldn't whip you. The pecan leaves began to rattle; Billy Bob slid slowly to the ground, and Aunt El, rushing her fingers through his hair, pulled him against her. Aw, Ma, he said, Aw, Ma.

After supper Billy Bob came and flung himself on the foot of my bed. He smelled all sour and sweet, the way boys do, and I felt very sorry for him, especially because he looked so worried. His eyes were almost shut with worry. You're s'posed to send sick folks flowers, he said righteously. About this time we heard the victrola, a lilting faraway sound, and a night moth flew through the window, drifting in the air delicate as the music. But it was dark now, and we couldn't tell if Miss Bobbit was dancing. Billy Bob, as though he were in pain, doubled up on the bed like a jackknife; but his face was suddenly clear, his grubby boy-eyes twitching like candles. She's so cute, he whispered, she's the cutest dickens I ever saw, gee, to hell with it, I don't care, I'd pick all the roses in China.

Preacher would have picked all the roses in China, too. He was as crazy about her as Billy Bob. But Miss Bobbit did not notice them. The sole communication we had with her was a note to Aunt El thanking her for the flowers. Day after day she sat on her porch, always dressed to beat the band, and doing a piece of embroidery, or combing curls in her hair, or reading a Webster's dictionary – formal, but friendly enough; if you said good-day to her she said good-day to you. Even so, the boys never could seem to get up the nerve to go over and talk with her, and most of the time she simply looked through them, even when they tomcatted up and down the street trying to get her eye. They wrestled, played Tarzan, did foolheaded bicycle tricks. It was a sorry business. A great many girls in town strolled by the Sawyer house two and three times within an hour just on the chance of getting a look. Some of the girls who did this were: Cora McCall, Mary Murphy Jones, Janice Ackerman. Miss Bobbit did not show any interest in them either. Cora would not speak to Billy Bob any more. The same was true with Janice and Preacher. As a matter of fact, Janice wrote Preacher a letter in red ink on lace-trimmed paper in which she told him he was vile beyond all human beings and words, that she considered their engagement broken, that he could have back the stuffed squirrel he'd given her. Preacher, saying he wanted to act nice, stopped her the next time she passed our house, and said, well, hell, she could keep that old squirrel if she wanted to. Afterwards, he couldn't understand why Janice ran away bawling the way she did.

Then one day the boys were being crazier than usual; Billy Bob was sagging around in his daddy's World War khakis, and Preacher, stripped to the waist, had a naked woman drawn on his chest with one of Aunt El's old lipsticks. They looked like perfect fools, but Miss Bobbit, reclining in a swing, merely yawned. It was noon, and there was no one passing in the street, except a colored girl, baby-fat and sugar-plum shaped, who hummed along carrying a pail of blackberries. But the boys, teasing at her like gnats, joined hands and wouldn't let her go by, not until she paid a tariff. I ain't studyin' no tariff, she said, what kinda tariff you talkin' about, mister? A party in the barn, said Preacher, between clenched teeth, mighty nice party in the barn. And she, with a sulky shrug, said, huh, she intended studyin' no barn parties. Whereupon Billy Bob capsized her berry pail, and when she, with despairing, piglike shrieks, bent down in futile gestures of rescue, Preacher, who can be mean as the devil, gave her behind a kick which sent her sprawling jellylike among the blackberries and the dust. Miss Bobbit came tearing across the road, her finger wagging like a metronome; like a schoolteacher she clapped her hands, stamped her foot, said: 'It is a well-known fact that gentlemen are put on the face of this earth for the protection of ladies. Do you suppose boys behave this way in towns like Memphis, New York, London, Hollywood or Paris?' The boys hung back, and shoved their hands in their pockets. Miss Bobbit helped the colored girl to her feet; she dusted her off, dried her eyes, held out a handkerchief and told her to blow. 'A pretty pass,' she said, 'a fine situation when a lady can't walk safely in the public daylight.'

Then the two of them went back and sat on Mrs Sawyer's porch; and for the next year they were never far apart, Miss Bobbit and this baby elephant, whose name was Rosalba Cat. At first, Mrs Sawyer raised a fuss about Rosalba being so much at her house. She told Aunt El that it went against the grain to have a nigger lolling smack there in plain sight on her front porch. But Miss Bobbit had a certain magic, whatever she did she did it with completeness, and so directly, so solemnly, that there was nothing to do but accept it. For instance, the tradespeople in town used to snicker when they called her *Miss* Bobbit; but by and by she was Miss Bobbit, and they gave her stiff little bows as she whirled by spinning her parasol. Miss Bobbit told everyone that Rosalba was her sister, which caused a good many jokes; but like most of her ideas, it gradually seemed natural, and when we would overhear them calling each other Sister Rosalba and Sister Bobbit none of us cracked a smile. But Sister Rosalba and Sister Bobbit did some queer things. There was the business about the dogs. Now there are a great many dogs in this town, rat terriers, bird dogs, bloodhounds; they trail along the forlorn noonhot streets in sleepy herds of six to a dozen, all waiting only for dark and the moon, when straight through the lonesome hours you can hear them howling: someone is dying, someone is dead. Miss Bobbit complained to the Sheriff; she said that certain of the dogs always planted themselves under her window, and that she was a light sleeper to begin with; what is more, and as Sister Rosalba said, she did not believe they were dogs at all, but some kind of devil. Naturally the Sheriff did nothing; and so she took the matter into her own hands. One morning, after an especially loud night, she was seen stalking through the town with Rosalba at her side, Rosalba carrying a flower basket filled with rocks; whenever they saw a dog they paused while Miss Bobbit scrutinized him. Sometimes she would shake her head, but more often she said, 'Yes, that's one of them, Sister Rosalba,' and Sister Rosalba, with ferocious aim, would take a rock from her basket and crack the dog between the eyes.

Another thing that happened concerns Mr Henderson. Mr Henderson has a back room in the Sawyer house; a tough runt of a man who formerly was a wildcat oil prospector in Oklahoma, he is about seventy years old and, like a lot of old men, obsessed by functions of the body. Also, he is a terrible drunk. One time he had been drunk for two weeks; whenever he heard Miss Bobbit and Sister Rosalba moving around the house, he would charge to the top of the stairs and bellow down to Mrs Sawyer that there were midgets in the walls trying to get at his supply of toilet paper. They've already stolen fifteen cents' worth, he said. One evening, when the two girls were sitting under a tree in the yard, Mr Henderson, sporting nothing more than a nightshirt, stamped out after them. Steal all my toilet paper, will you? he hollered, I'll show you midgets . . . Somebody come help me, else these midget bitches are liable to make off with every sheet in town. It was Billy Bob and Preacher who caught Mr Henderson and held him until some grown men arrived and began to tie him up. Miss Bobbit, who had behaved with admirable calm, told the men they did not know how to tie a proper knot, and undertook to do so herself. She did such a good job that all the circulation stopped in Mr Henderson's hands and feet and it was a month before he could walk again.

It was shortly afterwards that Miss Bobbit paid us a call. She came on Sunday and I was there alone, the family having gone to church. 'The odors of a church are so offensive,' she said, leaning forward and with her hands folded primly before her. 'I don't want you to think I'm a heathen, Mr C.; I've had enough experience to know that there is a God and that there is a Devil. But the way to tame the Devil is not to go down there to church and listen to what a sinful mean fool he is. No, love the Devil like you love Jesus: because he is a powerful man, and will do you a good turn if he knows you trust him. He has frequently done me good turns, like at dancing school in Memphis . . . I always called in the Devil to help me get the biggest part in our annual show. That is common sense; you see, I knew Jesus wouldn't have any truck with dancing. Now, as a matter of fact, I have called in the Devil just recently. He is the only one who can help me get out of this town. Not that I live here, not exactly. I think always about somewhere else, somewhere else where everything is dancing, like people dancing in the streets, and everything is pretty, like children on their birthdays. My precious papa said I live in the sky, but if he'd lived more in the sky he'd be rich like he wanted to be. The trouble with my papa was he did not love the Devil, he let the Devil love him. But I am very smart in that respect; I know the next best thing is very often the best. It was the next best thing for us to move to this town; and since I can't pursue my career here, the next best thing for me is to start a little business on the side. Which is what I have done. I am sole subscription agent in this county for an impressive list of magazines, including *Reader's Digest*, *Popular Mechanics*, *Dime Detective* and *Child's Life*. To be sure, Mr C., I'm not here to sell you anything. But I have a thought in mind. I was thinking those two boys that are always hanging around here, it occurred to me that they are men, after all. Do you suppose they would make a pair of likely assistants?'

Billy Bob and Preacher worked hard for Miss Bobbit, and for Sister Rosalba, too. Sister Rosalba carried a line of cosmetics called Dewdrop, and it was part of the boys' job to deliver purchases to her customers. Billy Bob used to be so tired in the evening he could hardly chew his supper. Aunt El said it was a shame and a pity, and finally one day when Billy Bob came down with a touch of sunstroke she said, all right, that settled it, Billy Bob would just have to quit Miss Bobbit. But Billy Bob cussed her out until his daddy had to lock him in his room; whereupon he said he was going to kill himself. Some cook we'd had told him once that if you ate a mess of collards all slopped over with molasses it would kill you sure as shooting; and so that is what he did. I'm dying, he said, rolling back and forth on his bed, I'm dying and nobody cares.

Miss Bobbit came over and told him to hush up. 'There's nothing wrong with you, boy,' she said. 'All you've got is a stomach ache.' Then she did something that shocked Aunt El very much: she stripped the covers off Billy Bob and rubbed him down with alcohol from head to toe. When Aunt El told her she did not think that was a nice thing for a little girl to do, Miss Bobbit replied: 'I don't know whether it's nice or not, but it's certainly very refreshing.' After which Aunt El did all she could to keep Billy Bob from going back to work for her, but his daddy said to leave him alone, they would have to let the boy lead his own life.

Miss Bobbit was very honest about money. She paid Billy Bob and Preacher their exact commission, and she would never let them treat her, as they often tried to do, at the drugstore or to the picture show. 'You'd better save your money,' she told them. 'That is, if you want to go to college. Because neither one of you has got the brains to win a scholarship, not even a football scholarship.' But it was over money that Billy Bob and Preacher had a big falling out; that was not the real reason, of course: the real reason was that they had grown cross-eyed jealous over Miss Bobbit. So one day, and he had the gall to do this right in front of Billy Bob, Preacher said to Miss Bobbit that she'd better check her accounts carefully because he had more than a suspicion that Billy Bob wasn't turning over to her *all* the money he collected. That's a damned lie, said Billy Bob, and with a clean left hook he knocked Preacher off the Sawyer porch and jumped after him into a bed of nasturtiums. But once Preacher got a hold on him, Billy Bob didn't stand a chance. Preacher even rubbed dirt in his eyes. During all this, Mrs Sawyer, leaning out an upper-story window, screamed like an eagle, and Sister Rosalba, fatly cheerful, ambiguously shouted, Kill him! Kill him! Kill him! Only Miss Bobbit seemed to know what she was doing. She plugged in the lawn hose, and gave the boys a close-up, blinding bath. Gasping, Preacher staggered to his feet. Oh, honey, he said, shaking himself like a wet dog, honey, you've got to decide. 'Decide *what*?' said Miss Bobbit, right away in a huff. Oh, honey, wheezed Preacher, you don't want us boys killing each other. You got to decide who is your real true sweetheart. 'Sweetheart, my eye,' said Miss Bobbit. 'I should've known better than to get myself involved with a lot of country children. What sort of businessman are you going to make? Now, you listen here, Preacher Star: I don't want a sweetheart, and if I did, it wouldn't be you. As a matter of fact, you don't even get up when a lady enters the room.'

Preacher spit on the ground and swaggered over to Billy Bob. Come on, he said, just as though nothing had happened, she's a hard one, she is, she don't want nothing but to make trouble between two good friends. For a moment it looked as if Billy Bob was going to join him in a peaceful togetherness; but suddenly, coming to his senses, he drew back and made a gesture. The boys regarded each other a full minute, all the closeness between them turning an ugly color: you can't hate so much unless you love, too. And Preacher's face showed all of this. But there was nothing for him to do except go away. Oh, yes, Preacher, you looked so lost that day that for the first time I really liked you, so skinny and mean and lost going down the road all by yourself.

They did not make it up, Preacher and Billy Bob; and it was not because they didn't want to, it was only that there did not seem to be any straight way for their friendship to happen again. But they couldn't get rid of this friendship: each was always aware of what the other was up to; and when Preacher found himself a new buddy, Billy Bob moped around for days, picking things up, dropping them again, or doing sudden wild things, like purposely poking his finger in the electric fan. Sometimes in the evenings Preacher would pause by the gate and talk with Aunt El. It was only to torment Billy Bob, I suppose, but he stayed friendly with all of us, and at Christmas time he gave us a huge box of shelled peanuts. He left a present for Billy Bob, too. It turned out to be a book of Sherlock Holmes; and on the flyleaf there was scribbled, 'Friends Like Ivy On the Wall Must Fall.' That's the corniest thing I ever saw, Billy Bob said. Jesus, what a dope he is! But then, and though it was a cold winter day, he went in the backyard and climbed up into the pecan tree, crouching there all afternoon in the blue December branches.

But most of the time he was happy, because Miss Bobbit

was there, and she was always sweet to him now. She and Sister Rosalba treated him like a man; that is to say, they allowed him to do everything for them. On the other hand, they let him win at three-handed bridge, they never questioned his lies, nor discouraged his ambitions. It was a happy while. However, trouble started again when school began. Miss Bobbit refused to go. 'It's ridiculous,' she said, when one day the principal, Mr Copland, came around to investigate, 'really ridiculous; I can read and write and there are *some* people in this town who have every reason to know that I can count money. No, Mr Copland, consider for a moment and you will see neither of us has the time nor energy. After all, it would only be a matter of whose spirit broke first, yours or mine. And besides, what is there for you to teach me? Now, if you knew anything about dancing, that would be another matter; but under the circumstances, yes, Mr Copland, under the circumstances, I suggest we forget the whole thing.' Mr Copland was perfectly willing to. But the rest of the town thought she ought to be whipped. Horace Deasley wrote a piece in the paper which was titled 'A Tragic Situation'. It was, in his opinion, a tragic situation when a small girl could defy what he, for some reason, termed the Constitution of the United States. The article ended with a question: *Can she get away with it?* She did; and so did

Sister Rosalba. Only she was colored, so no one cared. Billy Bob was not as lucky. It was school for him, all right; but he might as well have stayed home for the good it did him. On his first report card he got three F's, a record of some sort. But he is a smart boy. I guess he just couldn't live through those hours without Miss Bobbit; away from her he always seemed half-asleep. He was always in a fight, too; either his eye was black, or his lip was split, or his walk had a limp. He never talked about these fights, but Miss Bobbit was shrewd enough to guess the reason why. 'You are a dear, I know, I know. And I appreciate you, Billy Bob. Only don't fight with people because of me. Of course they say mean things about me. But do you know why that is, Billy Bob? It's a compliment, kind of. Because deep down they think I'm absolutely wonderful.'

And she was right: if you are not admired no one will take the trouble to disapprove. But actually we had no idea of how wonderful she was until there appeared the man known as Manny Fox. This happened late in February. The first news we had of Manny Fox was a series of jovial placards posted up in the stores around town: Manny Fox Presents the Fan Dancer Without the Fan; then, in smaller print: Also, Sensational Amateur Program Featuring Your Own Neighbors – First Prize, A Genuine Hollywood Screen Test. All this was to take place the following Thursday. The tickets were priced at one dollar each, which around here is a lot of money; but it is not often that we get any kind of flesh entertainment, so everybody shelled out their money and made a great to-do over the whole thing. The drugstore cowboys talked dirty all week, mostly about the fan dancer without the fan, who turned out to be Mrs Manny Fox. They stayed down the highway at the Chucklewood Tourist Camp; but they were in town all day, driving around in an old Packard which had Manny Fox's full name stenciled on all four doors. His wife was a deadpan pimento-tongued redhead with wet lips and moist eyelids; she was quite large actually, but compared to Manny Fox she seemed rather frail, for he was a fat cigar of a man.

They made the pool hall their headquarters, and every afternoon you could find them there, drinking beer and joking with the town loafs. As it developed, Manny Fox's business affairs were not restricted to theatrics. He also ran a kind of employment bureau: slowly he let it be known that for a fee of $150 he could get for any adventurous boys in the county high-class jobs working on fruit ships sailing from New Orleans to South America. The chance of a lifetime, he called it. There are not two boys around here who readily lay their hands on so much as five dollars; nevertheless, a

good dozen managed to raise the money. Ada Willing-
ham took all she'd saved to buy an angel tombstone for
her husband and gave it to her son, and Acey Trump's
papa sold an option on his cotton crop.

But the night of the show! That was a night when all
was forgotten: mortgages, and the dishes in the kitchen
sink. Aunt El said you'd think we were going to the opera,
everybody so dressed up, so pink and sweet-smelling.
The Odeon had not been so full since the night they
gave away the matched set of sterling silver. Practically
everybody had a relative in the show, so there was a lot
of nervousness to contend with. Miss Bobbit was the
only contestant we knew real well. Billy Bob couldn't sit
still; he kept telling us over and over that we mustn't
applaud for anybody but Miss Bobbit; Aunt El said that
would be very rude, which sent Billy Bob off into a state
again; and when his father bought us all bags of pop-
corn he wouldn't touch his because it would make his
hands greasy, and please, another thing, we mustn't be
noisy and eat ours while Miss Bobbit was performing.
That she was to be a contestant had come as a last-
minute surprise. It was logical enough, and there were
signs that should've told us; the fact, for instance, that
she had not set foot outside the Sawyer house in how
many days? And the victrola going half the night, her
shadow whirling on the window shade, and the secret,

stuffed look on Sister Rosalba's face whenever asked after Sister Bobbit's health. So there was her name on the program, listed second, in fact, though she did not appear for a long while. First came Manny Fox, greased and leering, who told a lot of peculiar jokes, clapping his hands, ha, ha. Aunt El said if he told another joke like that she was going to walk straight out: he did, and she didn't. Before Miss Bobbit came on there were eleven contestants, including Eustacia Bernstein, who imitated movie stars so that they all sounded like Eustacia, and there was an extraordinary Mr Buster Riley, a jug-eared old wool-hat from way in the back country who played 'Waltzing Matilda' on a saw. Up to that point, he was the hit of the show; not that there was any marked difference in the various receptions, for everybody applauded generously, everybody, that is, except Preacher Star. He was sitting two rows ahead of us, greeting each act with a donkey-loud boo. Aunt El said she was never going to speak to him again. The only person he ever applauded was Miss Bobbit. No doubt the Devil was on her side, but she deserved it. Out she came, tossing her hips, her curls, rolling her eyes. You could tell right away it wasn't going to be one of her classical numbers. She tapped across the stage, daintily holding up the sides of a cloud-blue skirt. That's the cutest thing I ever saw, said Billy Bob, smacking his thigh, and Aunt El had to agree that Miss Bobbit looked real sweet. When she started to twirl the whole audience broke into spontaneous applause; so she did it all over again, hissing, 'Faster, faster,' at poor Miss Adelaide, who was at the piano doing her Sunday-school best. 'I was born in China, and raised in Jay-pan . . .' We had never heard her sing before, and she had a rowdy sandpaper voice. '. . . if you don't like my peaches, stay away from my can, o-ho o-ho!' Aunt El gasped; she gasped again when Miss Bobbit, with a bump, up-ended her skirt to display blue-lace underwear, thereby collecting most of the whistles the boys had been saving for the fan dancer without the fan, which was just as well, as it later turned out, for that lady, to the tune of 'An Apple for the Teacher' and cries of gyp gyp, did her routine attired in a bathing suit. But showing off her bottom was not Miss Bobbit's final triumph. Miss Adelaide commenced an ominous thundering in the darker keys, at which point Sister Rosalba, carrying a lighted Roman candle, rushed onstage and handed it to Miss Bobbit, who was in the midst of a full split; she made it, too, and just as she did the Roman candle burst into fiery balls of red, white and blue, and we all had to stand up because she was singing 'The Star Spangled Banner' at the top of her lungs. Aunt El said afterwards that it was one of the most gorgeous things she'd ever seen on the American stage.

Well, she surely did deserve a Hollywood screen test and, inasmuch as she won the contest, it looked as though she were going to get it. Manny Fox said she was: honey, he said, you're real star stuff. Only he skipped town the next day, leaving nothing but hearty promises. Watch the mails, my friends, you'll all be hearing from me. That is what he said to the boys whose money he'd taken, and that is what he said to Miss Bobbit. There are three deliveries daily, and this sizable group gathered at the post office for all of them, a jolly crowd growing gradually joyless. How their hands trembled when a letter slid into their mailbox. A terrible hush came over them as the days passed. They all knew what the other was thinking, but no one could bring himself to say it, not even Miss Bobbit. Postmistress Patterson said it plainly, however: the man's a crook, she said, I knew he was a crook to begin with, and if I have to look at your faces one more day I'll shoot myself.

Finally, at the end of two weeks, it was Miss Bobbit who broke the spell. Her eyes had grown more vacant than anyone had ever supposed they might, but one day, after the last mail was up, all her old sizzle came back. 'O.K., boys, it's lynch law now,' she said, and proceeded to herd the whole troupe home with her. This was the first meeting of the Manny Fox Hangman's Club, an organization which, in a more social form, endures to this day, though Manny Fox has long since been caught and, so to say, hung. Credit for this went quite properly to Miss Bobbit. Within a week she'd written over three hundred descriptions of Manny Fox and dispatched them to Sheriffs throughout the South; she also wrote letters to papers in the larger cities, and these attracted wide attention. As a result, four of the robbed boys were offered good-paying jobs by the United Fruit Company, and late this spring, when Manny Fox was arrested in Uphigh, Arkansas, where he was pulling the same old dodge, Miss Bobbit was presented with a Good Deed Merit award from the Sunbeam Girls of America. For some reason, she made a point of letting the world know that this did not exactly thrill her. 'I do not approve of the organization,' she said. 'All that rowdy bugle blowing. It's neither good-hearted nor truly feminine. And anyway, what is a good deed? Don't let anybody fool you, a good deed is something you do because you want something in return.' It would be reassuring to report she was wrong, and that her just reward, when at last it came, was given out of kindness and love. However, this is not the case. About a week ago the boys involved in the swindle all received from Manny Fox checks covering their losses, and Miss Bobbit, with clodhopping determination, stalked into a meeting of the Hangman's Club, which is now an excuse for drinking beer and playing poker every Thursday night. 'Look, boys,' she said, laying it on the line, 'none of you ever thought to see that money again, but now that you have, you ought to invest it in something practical – like me.' The proposition was that they should pool their money and finance her trip to Hollywood; in return, they would get ten percent of her life's earnings which, after she was a star, and that would not be very long, would make them all rich men. 'At least,' as she said, 'in this part of the country.' Not one of the boys wanted to do it: but when Miss Bobbit looked at you, what was there to say?

Since Monday, it has been raining buoyant summer rain shot through with sun, but dark at night and full of sound, full of dripping leaves, watery chimings, sleepless scuttlings. Billy Bob is wide-awake, dry-eyed, though everything he does is a little frozen and his tongue is as stiff as a bell tongue. It has not been easy for him, Miss Bobbit's going. Because she'd meant more than that. Than what? Than being thirteen years old and crazy in love. She was the queer things in him, like the pecan tree and liking books and caring enough about people to let them hurt him. She was the things he was afraid to show anyone else. And in the dark the music trickled through the rain: won't there be nights when we will hear it just as though it were really there? And afternoons when the shadows will be all at once confused, and she will pass before us, unfurling across the lawn like a pretty piece of ribbon? She laughed to Billy Bob; she held his hand, she even kissed him. 'I'm not going to die,' she said. 'You'll come out there, and we'll climb a mountain, and we'll all live there together, you and me and Sister Rosalba.' But Billy Bob knew it would never happen that way, and so when the music came through the dark he would stuff the pillow over his head.

Only there was a strange smile about yesterday, and that was the day she was leaving. Around noon the sun came out, bringing with it into the air all the sweetness of wisteria. Aunt El's yellow Lady Anne's were blooming again, and she did something wonderful, she told Billy Bob he could pick them and give them to Miss Bobbit for goodbye. All afternoon Miss Bobbit sat on the porch surrounded by people who stopped by to wish her well. She looked as though she were going to Communion, dressed in white and with a white parasol. Sister Rosalba had given her a handkerchief, but she had to borrow it back because she couldn't stop blubbering. Another little girl brought a baked chicken, presumably to be eaten on the bus; the only trouble was she'd forgotten to take out the insides before cooking it. Miss Bobbit's mother said that was all right by her, chicken was chicken; which is memorable because it is the single opinion she ever voiced. There was only one sour note. For hours Preacher Star had been hanging around down at the corner, sometimes standing at the curb tossing a coin, and sometimes hiding behind a tree, as if he didn't want anyone to see him. It made everybody nervous. About twenty minutes before bus time he sauntered up and leaned against our gate. Billy Bob was still in the garden picking roses; by now he had enough for a bonfire, and their smell was as heavy as wind. Preacher stared at him until he lifted his head. As they looked at each other the rain began again, falling fine as sea spray and colored by a rainbow. Without a word, Preacher went over and started helping Billy Bob separate the roses into two giant bouquets: together they carried them to the curb. Across the street there were bumblebees of talk, but when Miss Bobbit saw them, two boys whose flower-masked faces were like yellow moons, she rushed down the steps, her arms outstretched. You could see what was going to happen; and we called out, our voices like lightning in the rain, but Miss Bobbit, running toward those moons of roses, did not seem to hear. That is when the six-o'clock bus ran over her.

A Christmas Memory

Imagine a morning in late November. A coming of winter morning more than twenty years ago. Consider the kitchen of a spreading old house in a country town. A great black stove is its main feature; but there is also a big round table and a fireplace with two rocking chairs placed in front of it. Just today the fireplace commenced its seasonal roar.

A woman with shorn white hair is standing at the kitchen window. She is wearing tennis shoes and a shapeless gray sweater over a summery calico dress. She is small and sprightly, like a bantam hen; but, due to a long youthful illness, her shoulders are pitifully hunched. Her face is remarkable – not unlike Lincoln's, craggy like that, and tinted by sun and wind; but it is delicate too, finely boned, and her eyes are sherry-colored and timid. 'Oh my,' she exclaims, her breath smoking the windowpane, 'it's fruitcake weather!'

The person to whom she is speaking is myself. I am

seven; she is sixty-something. We are cousins, very distant ones, and we have lived together – well, as long as I can remember. Other people inhabit the house, relatives; and though they have power over us, and frequently make us cry, we are not, on the whole, too much aware of them. We are each other's best friend. She calls me Buddy, in memory of a boy who was formerly her best friend. The other Buddy died in the 1880's, when she was still a child. She is still a child.

'I knew it before I got out of bed,' she says, turning away from the window with a purposeful excitement in her eyes. 'The courthouse bell sounded so cold and clear. And there were no birds singing; they've gone to warmer country, yes indeed. Oh, Buddy, stop stuffing biscuit and fetch our buggy. Help me find my hat. We've thirty cakes to bake.'

It's always the same: a morning arrives in November, and my friend, as though officially inaugurating the Christmas time of year that exhilarates her imagination and fuels the blaze of her heart, announces: 'It's fruit-cake weather! Fetch our buggy. Help me find my hat.'

The hat is found, a straw cartwheel corsaged with velvet roses out-of-doors has faded: it once belonged to a more fashionable relative. Together, we guide our buggy, a dilapidated baby carriage, out to the garden and into a grove of pecan trees. The buggy is mine; that is, it was bought for me when I was born. It is made of wicker, rather unraveled, and the wheels wobble like a drunkard's legs. But it is a faithful object; springtimes, we take it to the woods and fill it with flowers, herbs, wild fern for our porch pots; in the summer, we pile it with picnic paraphernalia and sugar-cane fishing poles and roll it down to the edge of a creek; it has its winter uses, too: as a truck for hauling firewood from the yard to the kitchen, as a warm bed for Queenie, our tough little orange and white rat terrier who has survived distemper and two rattlesnake bites. Queenie is trotting beside it now.

Three hours later we are back in the kitchen hulling a heaping buggyload of windfall pecans. Our backs hurt from gathering them: how hard they were to find (the main crop having been shaken off the trees and sold by the orchard's owners, who are not us) among the concealing leaves, the frosted, deceiving grass. Caarackle! A cheery crunch, scraps of miniature thunder sound as the shells collapse and the golden mound of sweet oily ivory meat mounts in the milk-glass bowl. Queenie begs to taste, and now and again my friend sneaks her a mite, though insisting we deprive ourselves. 'We mustn't, Buddy. If we start, we won't stop. And there's scarcely enough as there is. For thirty cakes.' The kitchen is growing dark. Dusk turns the window into a mirror: our reflections mingle with the rising moon as we work by the fireside in the firelight. At last, when the moon is quite high, we toss the final hull into the fire and, with joined sighs, watch it catch flame. The buggy is empty, the bowl is brimful.

We eat our supper (cold biscuits, bacon, blackberry jam) and discuss tomorrow. Tomorrow the kind of work I like best begins: buying. Cherries and citron, ginger and vanilla and canned Hawaiian pineapple, rinds and raisins and walnuts and whiskey and oh, so much flour, butter, so many eggs, spices, flavorings: why, we'll need a pony to pull the buggy home.

But before these purchases can be made, there is the question of money. Neither of us has any. Except for skinflint sums persons in the house occasionally provide (a dime is considered very big money); or what we earn ourselves from various activities: holding rummage sales, selling buckets of hand-picked blackberries, jars of homemade jam and apple jelly and peach preserves, rounding up flowers for funerals and weddings. Once we won seventy-ninth prize, five dollars, in a national football contest. Not that we know a fool thing about football. It's just that we enter any contest we hear about: at the moment our hopes are centered on the fifty-thousand-dollar Grand Prize being offered to name a new brand of coffee (we suggested 'A.M.'; and, after some hesitation, for my friend thought it perhaps sacrilegious, the slogan 'A.M.! Amen!'). To tell the truth, our only *really* profitable enterprise was the Fun and Freak Museum we conducted in a backyard woodshed two summers ago. The Fun was a stereopticon with slide views of Washington and New York lent us by a relative who had been to those places (she was furious when she discovered why we'd borrowed it); the Freak was a three-legged biddy chicken hatched by one of our own hens. Everybody hereabouts wanted to see that biddy: we charged grownups a nickel, kids two cents. And took in a good twenty dollars before the museum shut down due to the decease of the main attraction.

But one way and another we do each year accumulate Christmas savings, a Fruitcake Fund. These moneys we keep hidden in an ancient bead purse under a loose board under the floor under a chamber pot under my friend's bed. The purse is seldom removed from this safe location except to make a deposit, or, as happens every Saturday, a withdrawal; for on Saturdays I am allowed ten cents to go to the picture show. My friend has never been to a picture show, nor does she intend to: 'I'd rather hear you tell the story, Buddy. That way I can imagine it more. Besides, a person my age shouldn't squander their eyes. When the Lord comes, let me see him clear.' In addition to never having seen a movie, she has never: eaten in a restaurant, traveled more than five miles from home, received or sent a telegram, read anything except funny papers and the Bible, worn cosmetics, cursed, wished someone harm, told a lie on purpose, let a hungry dog go hungry. Here are a few things she has done, does do: killed with a hoe the biggest rattlesnake ever seen in this county (sixteen rattles), dip snuff (secretly), tame hummingbirds (just try it) till they balance on her finger, tell ghost stories (we both believe in ghosts) so tingling they chill you in July, talk to herself, take walks in the rain, grow the prettiest japonicas in town, know the recipe for every sort of old-time Indian cure, including a magical wart-remover.

Now, with supper finished, we retire to the room in a faraway part of the house where my friend sleeps in a scrap-quilt-covered iron bed painted rose pink, her favorite color. Silently, wallowing in the pleasures of conspiracy, we take the bead purse from its secret place and spill its contents on the scrap quilt. Dollar bills, tightly rolled and green as May buds. Somber fifty-cent pieces, heavy enough to weight a dead man's eyes. Lovely dimes, the liveliest coin, the one that really jingles. Nickels and quarters, worn smooth as creek pebbles. But mostly a hateful heap of bitter-odored pennies. Last summer others in the house contracted to pay us a penny for every twenty-five flies we killed. Oh, the carnage of August: the flies that flew to heaven! Yet it was

not work in which we took pride. And, as we sit counting pennies, it is as though we were back tabulating
dead flies. Neither of us has a head for figures; we count
slowly, lose track, start again. According to her calcula-
tions, we have $12.73. According to mine, exactly $13. 'I
do hope you're wrong, Buddy. We can't mess around
with thirteen. The cakes will fall. Or put somebody in the
cemetery. Why, I wouldn't dream of getting out of bed
on the thirteenth.' This is true: she always spends thirteenths in bed. So, to be on the safe side, we subtract a
penny and toss it out the window.

Of the ingredients that go into our fruitcakes, whiskey is the most expensive, as well as the hardest to
obtain: State laws forbid its sale. But everybody knows
you can buy a bottle from Mr Haha Jones. And the next
day, having completed our more prosaic shopping, we
set out for Mr Haha's business address, a 'sinful' (to
quote public opinion) fish-fry and dancing café down by
the river. We've been there before, and on the same
errand; but in previous years our dealings have been
with Haha's wife, an iodine-dark Indian woman with
brazzy peroxided hair and a dead-tired disposition.
Actually, we've never laid eyes on her husband, though
we've heard that he's an Indian too. A giant with razor
scars across his cheeks. They call him Haha because he's
so gloomy, a man who never laughs. As we approach

his café (a large log cabin festooned inside and out with chains of garish-gay naked lightbulbs and standing by the river's muddy edge under the shade of river trees where moss drifts through the branches like gray mist) our steps slow down. Even Queenie stops prancing and sticks close by. People have been murdered in Haha's café. Cut to pieces. Hit on the head. There's a case coming up in court next month. Naturally these goings-on happen at night when the colored lights cast crazy patterns and the victrola wails. In the daytime Haha's is shabby and deserted. I knock at the door, Queenie barks, my friend calls: 'Mrs Haha, ma'am? Anyone to home?'

Footsteps. The door opens. Our hearts overturn. It's Mr Haha Jones himself! And he *is* a giant; he *does* have scars; he *doesn't* smile. No, he glowers at us through Satan-tilted eyes and demands to know: 'What you want with Haha?'

For a moment we are too paralyzed to tell. Presently my friend half-finds her voice, a whispery voice at best: 'If you please, Mr Haha, we'd like a quart of your finest whiskey.'

His eyes tilt more. Would you believe it? Haha is smiling! Laughing, too. 'Which one of you is a drinkin' man?'

'It's for making fruitcakes, Mr Haha. Cooking.'

This sobers him. He frowns. 'That's no way to waste

good whiskey.' Nevertheless, he retreats into the shadowed café and seconds later appears carrying a bottle of daisy yellow unlabeled liquor. He demonstrates its sparkle in the sunlight and says: 'Two dollars.'

We pay him with nickels and dimes and pennies. Suddenly, jangling the coins in his hand like a fistful of dice, his face softens. 'Tell you what,' he proposes, pouring the money back into our bead purse, 'just send me one of them fruitcakes instead.'

'Well,' my friend remarks on our way home, 'there's a lovely man. We'll put an extra cup of raisins in *his* cake.'

The black stove, stoked with coal and firewood, glows like a lighted pumpkin. Eggbeaters whirl, spoons spin round in bowls of butter and sugar, vanilla sweetens the air, ginger spices it; melting, nose-tingling odors saturate the kitchen, suffuse the house, drift out to the world on puffs of chimney smoke. In four days our work is done. Thirty-one cakes, dampened with whiskey, bask on window sills and shelves.

Who are they for?

Friends. Not necessarily neighbor friends: indeed, the larger share are intended for persons we've met maybe once, perhaps not at all. People who've struck our fancy. Like President Roosevelt. Like the Reverend and Mrs J. C. Lucey, Baptist missionaries to Borneo who lectured here last winter. Or the little knife grinder

who comes through town twice a year. Or Abner
Packer, the driver of the six o'clock bus from Mobile,
who exchanges waves with us every day as he passes in
a dust-cloud whoosh. Or the young Wistons, a California couple whose car one afternoon broke down outside
the house and who spent a pleasant hour chatting with
us on the porch (young Mr Wiston snapped our picture,
the only one we've ever had taken). Is it because my
friend is shy with everyone *except* strangers that these
strangers, and merest acquaintances, seem to us our
truest friends? I think yes. Also, the scrapbooks we keep
of thank-you's on White House stationery, time-to-time
communications from California and Borneo, the knife
grinder's penny post cards, make us feel connected to
eventful worlds beyond the kitchen with its view of a
sky that stops.

Now a nude December fig branch grates against the
window. The kitchen is empty, the cakes are gone; yesterday we carted the last of them to the post office, where
the cost of stamps turned our purse inside out. We're
broke. That rather depresses me, but my friend insists
on celebrating – with two inches of whiskey left in Haha's
bottle. Queenie has a spoonful in a bowl of coffee (she
likes her coffee chicory-flavored and strong). The rest
we divide between a pair of jelly glasses. We're both
quite awed at the prospect of drinking straight whiskey;

the taste of it brings screwed-up expressions and sour shudders. But by and by we begin to sing, the two of us singing different songs simultaneously. I don't know the words to mine, just: *Come on along, come on along, to the dark-town strutters' ball.* But I can dance: that's what I mean to be, a tap dancer in the movies. My dancing shadow rollicks on the walls; our voices rock the chinaware; we giggle: as if unseen hands were tickling us. Queenie rolls on her back, her paws plow the air, something like a grin stretches her black lips. Inside myself, I feel warm and sparky as those crumbling logs, carefree as the wind in the chimney. My friend waltzes round the stove, the hem of her poor calico skirt pinched between her fingers as though it were a party dress: *Show me the way to go home*, she sings, her tennis shoes squeaking on the floor. *Show me the way to go home.*

Enter: two relatives. Very angry. Potent with eyes that scold, tongues that scald. Listen to what they have to say, the words tumbling together into a wrathful tune: 'A child of seven! whiskey on his breath! are you out of your mind? feeding a child of seven! must be loony! road to ruination! remember Cousin Kate? Uncle Charlie? Uncle Charlie's brother-in-law? shame! scandal! humiliation! kneel, pray, beg the Lord!'

Queenie sneaks under the stove. My friend gazes at her shoes, her chin quivers, she lifts her skirt and blows

43

her nose and runs to her room. Long after the town has gone to sleep and the house is silent except for the chimings of clocks and the sputter of fading fires, she is weeping into a pillow already as wet as a widow's handkerchief.

'Don't cry,' I say, sitting at the bottom of her bed and shivering despite my flannel nightgown that smells of last winter's cough syrup, 'don't cry,' I beg, teasing her toes, tickling her feet, 'you're too old for that.'

'It's because,' she hiccups, 'I *am* too old. Old and funny.'

'Not funny. Fun. More fun than anybody. Listen. If you don't stop crying you'll be so tired tomorrow we can't go cut a tree.'

She straightens up. Queenie jumps on the bed (where Queenie is not allowed) to lick her cheeks. 'I know where we'll find pretty trees, Buddy. And holly, too. With berries big as your eyes. It's way off in the woods. Farther than we've ever been. Papa used to bring us Christmas trees from there: carry them on his shoulder. That's fifty years ago. Well, now: I can't wait for morning.'

Morning. Frozen rime lusters the grass; the sun, round as an orange and orange as hot-weather moons, balances on the horizon, burnishes the silvered winter woods. A wild turkey calls. A renegade hog grunts in the undergrowth. Soon, by the edge of knee-deep, rapid-running water, we have to abandon the buggy. Queenie wades the stream first, paddles across barking complaints at the swiftness of the current, the pneumonia-making coldness of it. We follow, holding our shoes and equipment (a hatchet, a burlap sack) above our heads. A mile more: of chastising thorns, burs and briers that catch at our clothes; of rusty pine needles brilliant with gaudy fungus and molted feathers. Here, there, a flash, a flutter, an ecstasy of shrillings remind us that not all the birds have flown south. Always, the path unwinds through lemony sun pools and pitch vine tunnels. Another creek to cross: a disturbed armada of speckled trout froths the water round us, and frogs the size of plates practice belly flops; beaver workmen are building a dam. On the farther shore, Queenie shakes herself and trembles. My friend shivers, too: not with cold but enthusiasm. One of her hat's ragged roses sheds a petal as she lifts her head and inhales the pine-heavy air. 'We're almost there; can you smell it, Buddy?' she says, as though we were approaching an ocean.

And, indeed, it is a kind of ocean. Scented acres of holiday trees, prickly-leafed holly. Red berries shiny as Chinese bells: black crows swoop upon them screaming. Having stuffed our burlap sacks with enough greenery and crimson to garland a dozen windows, we set about choosing a tree. 'It should be,' muses my friend, 'twice as tall as a boy. So a boy can't steal the star.' The one we pick is twice as tall as me. A brave handsome brute that survives thirty hatchet strokes before it keels with a creaking, rending cry. Lugging it like a kill, we commence the long trek out. Every few yards we abandon the struggle, sit down and pant. But we have the strength of triumphant huntsmen; that and the tree's virile, icy perfume revive us, goad us on. Many compliments accompany our sunset return along the red clay road to town; but my friend is sly and noncommittal when passers-by praise the treasure perched on our buggy: what a fine tree and where did it come from? 'Yonderways,' she murmurs vaguely. Once a car stops and the rich mill owner's lazy wife leans out and whines: 'Giveya two-bits cash for that ol tree.' Ordinarily my friend is afraid of saying no; but on this occasion she promptly shakes her head: 'We wouldn't take a dollar.' The mill owner's wife persists. 'A dollar, my foot! Fifty cents. That's my last offer. Goodness, woman, you can get another one.' In answer, my friend gently reflects: 'I doubt it. There's never two of anything.'

Home: Queenie slumps by the fire and sleeps till tomorrow, snoring loud as a human.

A trunk in the attic contains: a shoebox of ermine tails (off the opera cape of a curious lady who once rented a room in the house), coils of frazzled tinsel gone gold with age, one silver star, a brief rope of dilapidated, undoubtedly dangerous candy-like light bulbs. Excellent decorations, as far as they go, which isn't far enough: my friend wants our tree to blaze 'like a Baptist window,' droop with weighty snows of ornament. But we can't afford the made-in-Japan splendors at the five-and-dime. So we do what we've always done: sit for days at the kitchen table with scissors and crayons and stacks of colored paper. I make sketches and my friend cuts them out: lots of cats, fish too (because they're easy to draw), some apples, some watermelons, a few winged angels devised from saved-up sheets of Hershey-bar tin foil. We use safety pins to attach these creations to the tree; as a final touch, we sprinkle the branches with shredded cotton (picked in August for this purpose). My friend, surveying the effect, clasps her hands together. 'Now honest, Buddy. Doesn't it look good enough to eat?' Queenie tries to eat an angel.

After weaving and ribboning holly wreaths for all the front windows, our next project is the fashioning of family gifts. Tie-dye scarves for the ladies, for the men a home-brewed lemon and licorice and aspirin syrup to be taken 'at the first Symptoms of a Cold and after Hunting.' But when it comes time for making each other's gift, my friend and I separate to work secretly.

I would like to buy her a pearl-handled knife, a radio, a whole pound of chocolate-covered cherries (we tasted some once, and she always swears: 'I could live on them, Buddy, Lord yes I could – and that's not taking His name in vain'). Instead, I am building her a kite. She would like to give me a bicycle (she's said so on several million occasions: 'If only I could, Buddy. It's bad enough in life to do without something *you* want; but confound it, what gets my goat is not being able to give somebody something you want *them* to have. Only one of these days I will, Buddy. Locate you a bike. Don't ask how. Steal it, maybe'). Instead, I'm fairly certain that she is building me a kite – the same as last year, and the year before: the year before that we exchanged slingshots. All of which is fine by me. For we are champion kite-fliers who study the wind like sailors; my friend, more accomplished than I, can get a kite aloft when there isn't enough breeze to carry clouds.

Christmas Eve afternoon we scrape together a nickel and go to the butcher's to buy Queenie's traditional gift, a good gnawable beef bone. The bone, wrapped in funny paper, is placed high in the tree near the silver star. Queenie knows it's there. She squats at the foot of the tree staring up in a trance of greed: when bedtime arrives she refuses to budge. Her excitement is equaled by my own. I kick the covers and turn my pillow as though it were a scorching summer's night. Somewhere a rooster crows: falsely, for the sun is still on the other side of the world.

'Buddy, are you awake?' It is my friend, calling from her room, which is next to mine; and an instant later she is sitting on my bed holding a candle. 'Well, I can't sleep a hoot,' she declares. 'My mind's jumping like a jack rabbit. Buddy, do you think Mrs Roosevelt will serve our cake at dinner?' We huddle in the bed, and she squeezes my hand I-love-you. 'Seems like your hand used to be so much smaller. I guess I hate to see you grow up. When you're grown up, will we still be friends?' I say always. 'But I feel so bad, Buddy. I wanted so bad to give you a bike. I tried to sell my cameo Papa gave me. Buddy' – she hesitates, as though embarrassed – 'I made you another kite.' Then I confess that I made her one, too; and we laugh. The candle burns too short to hold. Out it goes, exposing the starlight, the stars spinning at the window like a visible caroling that slowly, slowly daybreak silences. Possibly we doze; but the beginnings of dawn splash us like cold water: we're up, wide-eyed and wandering while we wait for others to waken. Quite deliberately my friend drops a kettle on the kitchen floor. I tap-dance in front of closed doors.

One by one the household emerges, looking as though they'd like to kill us both; but it's Christmas, so they can't. First, a gorgeous breakfast: just everything you can imagine – from flapjacks and fried squirrel to hominy grits and honey-in-the-comb. Which puts everyone in a good humor except my friend and I. Frankly, we're so impatient to get at the presents we can't eat a mouthful.

Well, I'm disappointed. Who wouldn't be? With socks, a Sunday school shirt, some handkerchiefs, a hand-me-down sweater and a year's subscription to a religious magazine for children. *The Little Shepherd*. It makes me boil. It really does.

My friend has a better haul. A sack of Satsumas, that's her best present. She is proudest, however, of a white wool shawl knitted by her married sister. But she *says* her favorite gift is the kite I built her. And it *is* very beautiful; though not as beautiful as the one she made me, which is blue and scattered with gold and green Good Conduct stars; moreover, my name is painted on it, 'Buddy'.

'Buddy, the wind is blowing.'

The wind is blowing, and nothing will do till we've run to a pasture below the house where Queenie has scooted to bury her bone (and where, a winter hence, Queenie will be buried, too). There, plunging through the healthy waist-high grass, we unreel our kites, feel them twitching at the string like sky fish as they swim into the wind. Satisfied, sun-warmed, we sprawl in the grass and peel Satsumas and watch our kites cavort. Soon I forget the socks and hand-me-down sweater. I'm as happy as if we'd already won the fifty-thousand-dollar Grand Prize in that coffee-naming contest.

'My, how foolish I am!' my friend cries, suddenly alert, like a woman remembering too late she has biscuits in the oven. 'You know what I've always thought?' she asks in a tone of discovery, and not smiling at me but a point beyond. 'I've always thought a body would have to be sick and dying before they saw the Lord. And I imagined that when He came it would be like looking at the Baptist window: pretty as colored glass with the sun pouring through, such a shine you don't know it's getting dark. And it's been a comfort: to think of that shine taking away all the spooky feeling. But I'll wager it never happens. I'll wager at the very end a body realizes the Lord has already shown Himself. That things as they are' – her hand circles in a gesture that gathers clouds and kites and grass and Queenie pawing earth over her bone – 'just what they've always seen, was seeing Him. As for me, I could leave the world with today in my eyes.'

*

This is our last Christmas together.

Life separates us. Those who Know Best decide that I belong in a military school. And so follows a miserable succession of bugle-blowing prisons, grim reveille-ridden summer camps. I have a new home too. But it doesn't count. Home is where my friend is, and there I never go.

And there she remains, puttering around the kitchen. Alone with Queenie. Then alone. ('Buddy dear,' she writes in her wild hard-to-read script, 'yesterday Jim Macy's horse kicked Queenie bad. Be thankful she didn't feel much. I wrapped her in a Fine Linen sheet and rode her in the buggy down to Simpson's pasture where she can be with all her Bones . . .') For a few Novembers she continues to bake her fruitcakes single-handed; not as many, but some: and, of course, she always sends me 'the best of the batch.' Also, in every letter she encloses a dime wadded in toilet paper: 'See a picture show and write me the story.' But gradually in her letters she tends to confuse me with her other friend, the Buddy who died in the 1880's; more and more thirteenths are not the only days she stays in bed: a morning arrives in November, a leafless birdless coming of winter morning, when she cannot rouse herself to exclaim: 'Oh my, it's fruitcake weather!'

And when that happens, I know it. A message saying

so merely confirms a piece of news some secret vein had already received, severing from me an irreplaceable part of myself, letting it loose like a kite on a broken string. That is why, walking across a school campus on this particular December morning, I keep searching the sky. As if I expected to see, rather like hearts, a lost pair of kites hurrying toward heaven.

A Tree of Night

It was winter. A string of naked lightbulbs, from which it seemed all warmth had been drained, illuminated the little depot's cold, windy platform. Earlier in the evening it had rained, and now icicles hung along the station-house eaves like some crystal monster's vicious teeth. Except for a girl, young and rather tall, the platform was deserted. The girl wore a gray flannel suit, a raincoat, and a plaid scarf. Her hair, parted in the middle and rolled up neatly on the sides, was rich blondish-brown; and, while her face tended to be too thin and narrow, she was, though not extraordinarily so, attractive. In addition to an assortment of magazines and a gray suede purse on which elaborate brass letters spelled Kay, she carried conspicuously a green Western guitar.

When the train, spouting steam and glaring with light, came out of the darkness and rumbled to a halt, Kay assembled her paraphernalia and climbed up into the last coach.

The coach was a relic with a decaying interior of ancient red-plush seats, bald in spots, and peeling iodine-colored woodwork. An old-time copper lamp, attached to the ceiling, looked romantic and out of place. Gloomy dead smoke sailed the air; and the car's heated closeness accentuated the stale odor of discarded sandwiches, apple cores, and orange hulls: this garbage, including Lily cups, soda-pop bottles, and mangled newspapers, littered the long aisle. From a water cooler, embedded in the wall, a steady stream trickled to the floor. The passengers, who glanced up wearily when Kay entered, were not, it seemed, at all conscious of any discomfort.

Kay resisted a temptation to hold her nose and threaded her way carefully down the aisle, tripping once, without disaster, over a dozing fat man's protruding leg. Two nondescript men turned an interested eye as she passed; and a kid stood up in his seat squalling, 'Hey, Mama, look at de banjo! Hey, lady, lemme play ya banjo!' till a slap from Mama quelled him.

There was only one empty place. She found it at the end of the car in an isolated alcove occupied already by a man and woman who were sitting with their feet settled lazily on the vacant seat opposite. Kay hesitated a second then said, 'Would you mind if I sat here?'

The woman's head snapped up as if she had not been asked a simple question, but stabbed with a needle, too.

Nevertheless, she managed a smile. 'Can't say as I see what's to stop you, honey,' she said, taking her feet down and also, with a curious impersonality, removing the feet of the man who was staring out the window, paying no attention whatsoever.

Thanking the woman, Kay took off her coat, sat down, and arranged herself with purse and guitar at her side, magazines in her lap: comfortable enough, though she wished she had a pillow for her back.

The train lurched; a ghost of steam hissed against the window; slowly the dingy lights of the lonesome depot faded past.

'Boy, what a jerkwater dump,' said the woman. 'No town, no nothin'.'

Kay said, 'The town's a few miles away.'

'That so? Live there?'

No. Kay explained she had been at the funeral of an uncle. An uncle who, though she did not of course mention it, had left her nothing in his will but the green guitar. Where was she going? Oh, back to college.

After mulling this over, the woman concluded, 'What'll you ever learn in a place like that? Let me tell you, honey, I'm plenty educated and I never saw the inside of no college.'

'You didn't?' murmured Kay politely and dismissed the matter by opening one of her magazines. The light was dim for reading and none of the stories looked in the least compelling. However, not wanting to become involved in a conversational marathon, she continued gazing at it stupidly till she felt a furtive tap on her knee.

'Don't read,' said the woman. 'I need somebody to talk to. Naturally, it's no fun talking to *him*.' She jerked a thumb toward the silent man. 'He's afflicted: deaf and dumb, know what I mean?'

Kay closed the magazine and looked at her more or less for the first time. She was short; her feet barely scraped the floor. And like many undersized people she had a freak of structure, in her case an enormous, really huge head. Rouge so brightened her sagging, flesh-featured face it was difficult even to guess at her age: perhaps fifty, fifty-five. Her big sheep eyes squinted, as if distrustful of what they saw. Her hair was an obviously dyed red, and twisted into parched, fat corkscrew curls. A once-elegant lavender hat of impressive size flopped crazily on the side of her head, and she was kept busy brushing back a drooping cluster of celluloid cherries sewed to the brim. She wore a plain, somewhat shabby blue dress. Her breath had a vividly sweetish gin smell.

'You do wanna talk to me, don't you honey?'

'Sure,' said Kay, moderately amused.

'Course you do. You bet you do. That's what I like about a train. Bus people are a close-mouthed buncha dopes. But a train's the place for putting your cards on the table, that's what I always say.' Her voice was cheerful and booming, husky as a man's. 'But on accounta *him*, I always try to get us this here seat; it's more private, like a swell compartment, see?'

'It's very pleasant,' Kay agreed. 'Thanks for letting me join you.'

'Only too glad to. We don't have much company; it makes some folks nervous to be around him.'

As if to deny it, the man made a queer, furry sound deep in his throat and plucked the woman's sleeve. 'Leave me alone, dearheart,' she said, as if she were talking to an inattentive child. 'I'm O.K. We're just having us a nice little ol' talk. Now behave yourself or this pretty girl will go away. She's very rich; she goes to college.' And winking, she added, 'He thinks I'm drunk.'

The man slumped in the seat, swung his head sideways, and studied Kay intently from the corners of his eyes. These eyes, like a pair of clouded milky-blue marbles, were thickly lashed and oddly beautiful. Now, except for a certain remoteness, his wide, hairless face had no real expression. It was as if he were incapable of experiencing or reflecting the slightest emotion. His gray hair was clipped close and combed forward into uneven bangs. He looked like a child aged abruptly by some uncanny method. He wore a frayed blue serge suit, and he had anointed himself with a cheap, vile perfume. Around his wrist was strapped a Mickey Mouse watch.

'He thinks I'm drunk,' the woman repeated. 'And the real funny part is, I am. Oh shoot – you gotta do something, ain't that right?' She bent closer. 'Say, ain't it?'

Kay was still gawking at the man; the way he was looking at her made her squeamish, but she could not take her eyes off him. 'I guess so,' she said.

'Then let's us have us a drink,' suggested the woman. She plunged her hand into an oilcloth satchel and pulled out a partially filled gin bottle. She began to unscrew the cap, but, seeming to think better of this, handed the bottle to Kay. 'Gee, I forgot about you being company,' she said. 'I'll go get us some nice paper cups.'

So, before Kay could protest that she did not want a drink, the woman had risen and started none too steadily down the aisle toward the water cooler.

Kay yawned and rested her forehead against the windowpane, her fingers idly strumming the guitar: the strings sang a hollow, lulling tune, as monotonously soothing as the Southern landscape, smudged in darkness, flowing past the window. An icy winter moon rolled above the train across the night sky like a thin white wheel.

And then, without warning, a strange thing happened: the man reached out and gently stroked Kay's cheek. Despite the breathtaking delicacy of this movement, it was such a bold gesture Kay was at first too startled to know what to make of it: her thoughts shot in three or four fantastic directions. He leaned forward till his queer eyes were very near her own; the reek of his perfume was sickening. The guitar was silent while they exchanged a searching gaze. Suddenly, from some spring of compassion, she felt for him a keen sense of pity; but also, and this she could not suppress, an overpowering disgust, an absolute loathing: something about him, an elusive quality she could not quite put a finger on, reminded her of – of what?

After a little, he lowered his hand solemnly and sank back in the seat, an asinine grin transfiguring his face, as if he had performed a clever stunt for which he wished applause.

'Giddyup! Giddyup! my little bucker-ROOS . . .' shouted the woman. And she sat down, loudly proclaiming to be, 'Dizzy as a witch! Dog tired! Whew!' From a handful of Lily cups she separated two and casually thrust the rest down her blouse. 'Keep 'em safe and dry, ha ha ha . . .' A coughing spasm seized her, but when it was over she appeared calmer. 'Has my boy friend been entertaining?' she asked, patting her bosom reverently. 'Ah, he's so sweet.' She looked as if she might pass out. Kay rather wished she would.

'I don't want a drink,' Kay said, returning the bottle. 'I never drink: I hate the taste.'

'Mustn't be a kill-joy,' said the woman firmly. 'Here now, hold your cup like a good girl.'

'No, please . . .'

'Formercysake, hold it still. Imagine, nerves at your age! Me, I can shake like a leaf, I've got reasons. Oh, Lordy, have I got 'em.'

'But . . .'

A dangerous smile tipped the woman's face hideously awry. 'What's the matter? Don't you think I'm good enough to drink with?'

'Please, don't misunderstand,' said Kay, a tremor in her voice. 'It's just that I don't like being forced to do something I don't want to. So look, couldn't I give this to the gentleman?'

'Him? No sirree: he needs what little sense he's got. Come on, honey, down the hatch.'

Kay, seeing it was useless, decided to succumb and avoid a possible scene. She sipped and shuddered. It was terrible gin. It burned her throat till her eyes watered. Quickly, when the woman was not watching, she emptied the cup out into the sound hole of the guitar. It happened, however, that the man saw; and Kay, realizing it, recklessly signaled to him with her eyes a plea not to give her away. But she could not tell from his clear-blank expression how much he understood.

'Where you from, kid?' resumed the woman presently.

For a bewildered moment, Kay was unable to provide an answer. The names of several cities came to her all at once. Finally, from this confusion, she extracted: 'New Orleans. My home is in New Orleans.'

The woman beamed. 'N.O.'s where I wanna go when I kick off. One time, oh, say 1923, I ran me a sweet little fortune-teller parlor there. Let's see, that was on St Peter Street.' Pausing, she stooped and set the empty gin bottle on the floor. It rolled into the aisle and rocked back and forth with a drowsy sound. 'I was raised in Texas – on a big ranch – my papa was rich. Us kids always had the best; even Paris, France, clothes. I'll bet you've got a big swell house, too. Do you have a garden? Do you grow flowers?'

'Just lilacs.'

A conductor entered the coach, preceded by a cold gust of wind that rattled the trash in the aisle and briefly livened the dull air. He lumbered along, stopping now and then to punch a ticket or talk with a passenger. It was after midnight. Someone was expertly playing a harmonica. Someone else was arguing the merits of a certain politician. A child cried out in his sleep.

'Maybe you wouldn't be so snotty if you knew who we was,' said the woman, bobbing her tremendous head. 'We ain't nobodies, not by a long shot.'

Embarrassed, Kay nervously opened a pack of cigarettes and lighted one. She wondered if there might not be a seat in a car up ahead. She could not bear the woman, or, for that matter, the man, another minute. But she had never before been in a remotely comparable situation. 'If you'll excuse me now,' she said, 'I have to be leaving. It's been very pleasant, but I promised to meet a friend on the train . . .'

With almost invisible swiftness the woman grasped the girl's wrist. 'Didn't your mama ever tell you it was sinful to lie?' she stage-whispered. The lavender hat tumbled off her head but she made no effort to retrieve it. Her tongue flicked out and wetted her lips. And, as Kay stood up, she increased the pressure of her grip. 'Sit down, dear . . . there ain't any friend . . . Why, we're your only friends and we wouldn't have you leave us for the world.'

'Honestly, I wouldn't lie.'

'Sit down, dear.'

Kay dropped her cigarette and the man picked it up.

He slouched in the corner and became absorbed in blowing a chain of lush smoke rings that mounted upward like hollow eyes and expanded into nothing.

'Why, you wouldn't want to hurt his feelings by leaving us, now, would you, dear?' crooned the woman softly. 'Sit down – down – now, that's a good girl. My, what a pretty guitar. What a pretty, pretty guitar . . .' Her voice faded before the sudden whooshing, static noise of a second train. And for an instant the lights in the coach went off; in the darkness the passing train's golden windows winked black-yellow-black-yellow-black-yellow. The man's cigarette pulsed like the glow of a firefly, and his smoke rings continued rising tranquilly. Outside, a bell pealed wildly.

When the lights came on again, Kay was massaging her wrist where the woman's strong fingers had left a painful bracelet mark. She was more puzzled than angry. She determined to ask the conductor if he would find her a different seat. But when he arrived to take her ticket, the request stuttered on her lips incoherently.

'Yes, miss?'

'Nothing,' she said.

And he was gone.

The trio in the alcove regarded one another in mysterious silence till the woman said, 'I've got something

65

here I wanna show you, honey.' She rummaged once more in the oilcloth satchel. 'You won't be so snotty after you get a gander at this.'

What she passed to Kay was a handbill, published on such yellowed, antique paper it looked as if it must be centuries old. In fragile, overly fancy lettering, it read:

LAZARUS

THE MAN WHO IS BURIED ALIVE
A MIRACLE
SEE FOR YOURSELF

Adults, 25¢ – Children, 10¢

'I always sing a hymn and read a sermon,' said the woman. 'It's awful sad: some folks cry, especially the old ones. And I've got me a perfectly elegant costume: a black veil and a black dress, oh, very becoming. *He* wears a gorgeous made-to-order bridegroom suit and a turban and lotsa talcum on his face. See, we try to make it as much like a bonafide funeral as we can. But shoot, nowadays you're likely to get just a buncha smart alecks come for laughs – so sometimes I'm real glad he's afflicted like he is on accounta otherwise his feelings would be hurt, maybe.'

Kay said, 'You mean you're with a circus or a side-show or something like that?'

'Nope, us alone,' said the woman as she reclaimed the fallen hat. 'We've been doing it for years and years – played every tank town in the South: Singasong, Mississippi – Spunky, Louisiana – Eureka, Alabama ...' These and other names rolled off her tongue musically, running together like rain. 'After the hymn, after the sermon, we bury him.'

'In a coffin?'

'Sort of. It's gorgeous, it's got silver stars painted all over the lid.'

'I should think he would suffocate,' said Kay, amazed. 'How long does he stay buried?'

'All told it takes maybe an hour – course that's not counting the lure.'

'The lure?'

'Uh huh. It's what we do the night before the show. See, we hunt up a store, any ol' store with a big glass window'll do, and get the owner to let *him* sit inside this window, and, well, hypnotize himself. Stays there all night stiff as a poker and people come and look: scares the livin' hell out of 'em ...' While she talked she jiggled a finger in her ear, withdrawing it occasionally to examine her find. 'And one time this ol' bindle-stiff Mississippi sheriff tried to ...'

The tale that followed was baffling and pointless: Kay did not bother to listen. Nevertheless, what she had heard already inspired a reverie, a vague recapitulation of her uncle's funeral; an event which, to tell the truth, had not much affected her since she had scarcely known him. And so, while gazing abstractedly at the man, an image of her uncle's face, white next the pale silk casket pillow, appeared in her mind's eye. Observing their faces simultaneously, both the man's and uncle's, as it were, she thought she recognized an odd parallel: there was about the man's face the same kind of shocking, embalmed, secret stillness, as though, in a sense, he were truly an exhibit in a glass cage, complacent to be seen, uninterested in seeing.

'I'm sorry, what did you say?'

'I said: I sure wish they'd lend us the use of a regular cemetery. Like it is now we have to put on the show wherever we can . . . mostly in empty lots that are nine times outa ten smack up against some smelly fillin' station, which ain't exactly a big help. But like I say, we got us a swell act, the best. You oughta come see it if you get a chance.'

'Oh, I should love to,' Kay said, absently.

'Oh, I should love to,' mimicked the woman. 'Well, who asked you? Anybody ask you?' She hoisted up her skirt and enthusiastically blew her nose on the ragged hem of a petticoat. 'Bu-leeve me, it's a hard way to turn a dollar. Know what our take was last month? Fifty-three bucks! Honey, you try living on that sometime.' She sniffed and rearranged her skirt with considerable primness. 'Well, one of these days my sweet boy's sure enough going to die down there; and even then somebody'll say it was a gyp.'

At this point the man took from his pocket what seemed to be a finely shellacked peach seed and balanced it on the palm of his hand. He looked across at Kay and, certain of her attention, opened his eyelids wide and began to squeeze and caress the seed in an undefinably obscene manner.

Kay frowned. 'What does he want?'

'He wants you to buy it.'

'But what is it?'

'A charm,' said the woman. 'A love charm.'

Whoever was playing the harmonica stopped. Other sounds, less unique, became at once prominent: someone snoring, the gin bottle seesaw rolling, voices in sleepy argument, the train wheels' distant hum.

'Where could you get love cheaper, honey?'

'It's nice. I mean it's cute . . .' Kay said, stalling for time. The man rubbed and polished the seed on his trouser leg. His head was lowered at a supplicating, mournful angle, and presently he stuck the seed between his teeth and bit it, as if it were a suspicious piece of silver. 'Charms always bring me bad luck. And besides . . . please, can't you make him stop acting that way?'

'Don't look so scared,' said the woman, more flat-voiced than ever. 'He ain't gonna hurt you.'

'Make him stop, damn it!'

'What can I do?' asked the woman, shrugging her shoulders. 'You're the one that's got money. You're rich. All he wants is a dollar, one dollar.'

Kay tucked her purse under her arm. 'I have just enough to get back to school,' she lied, quickly rising and stepping out into the aisle. She stood there a moment, expecting trouble. But nothing happened.

The woman, with rather deliberate indifference, heaved a sigh and closed her eyes; gradually the man subsided and stuck the charm back in his pocket. Then his hand crawled across the seat to join the woman's in a lax embrace.

Kay shut the door and moved to the front of the observation platform. It was bitterly cold in the open air, and she had left her raincoat in the alcove. She loosened her scarf and draped it over her head.

Although she had never made this trip before, the train was traveling through an area strangely familiar: tall trees, misty, painted pale by malicious moonshine, towered steep on either side without a break or clearing.

Above, the sky was a stark, unexplorable blue thronged with stars that faded here and there. She could see streamers of smoke trailing from the train's engine like long clouds of ectoplasm. In one corner of the platform a red kerosene lantern cast a colorful shadow.

She found a cigarette and tried to light it: the wind snuffed match after match till only one was left. She walked to the corner where the lantern burned and cupped her hands to protect the last match: the flame caught, sputtered, died. Angrily she tossed away the cigarette and empty folder; all the tension in her tightened to an exasperating pitch and she slammed the wall with her fist and began to whimper softly, like an irritable child.

The intense cold made her head ache, and she longed to go back inside the warm coach and fall asleep. But she couldn't, at least not yet; and there was no sense in wondering why, for she knew the answer very well. Aloud, partly to keep her teeth from chattering and partly because she needed the reassurance of her own voice, she said: 'We're in Alabama now, I think, and tomorrow we'll be in Atlanta and I'm nineteen and I'll be twenty in August and I'm a sophomore . . .' She glanced around at the darkness, hoping to see a sign of dawn, and finding the same endless wall of trees, the same frosty moon. 'I hate him, he's horrible and I hate him . . .' She stopped, ashamed of her foolishness and too tired to evade the truth: she was afraid.

Suddenly she felt an eerie compulsion to kneel down and touch the lantern. Its graceful glass funnel was warm, and the red glow seeped through her hands, making them luminous. The heat thawed her fingers and tingled along her arms.

She was so preoccupied she did not hear the door open. The train wheels roaring clickety-clack-clackety-click hushed the sound of the man's footsteps.

It was a subtle zero sensation that warned her finally; but some seconds passed before she dared look behind.

He was standing there with mute detachment, his head tilted, his arms dangling at his sides. Staring up into his harmless, vapid face, flushed brilliant by the lantern light, Kay knew of what she was afraid: it was a memory, a childish memory of terrors that once, long ago, had hovered above her like haunted limbs on a tree of night. Aunts, cooks, strangers – each eager to spin a tale or teach a rhyme of spooks and death, omens, spirits, demons. And always there had been the unfailing threat of the wizard man: stay close to the house, child, else a wizard man'll snatch you and eat you alive! He lived everywhere, the wizard man, and everywhere was danger. At night, in bed, hear him tapping at the window? Listen!

Holding onto the railing, she inched upward till she was standing erect. The man nodded and waved his hand toward the door. Kay took a deep breath and stepped forward. Together they went inside.

The air in the coach was numb with sleep: a solitary light now illuminated the car, creating a kind of artificial dusk. There was no motion but the train's sluggish sway, and the stealthy rattle of discarded newspapers.

The woman alone was wide awake. You could see she was greatly excited: she fidgeted with her curls and celluloid cherries, and her plump little legs, crossed at the ankles, swung agitatedly back and forth. She paid no attention when Kay sat down. The man settled in the seat with one leg tucked beneath him and his arms folded across his chest.

In an effort to be casual, Kay picked up a magazine. She realized the man was watching her, not removing his gaze an instant: she knew this though she was afraid to confirm it, and she wanted to cry out and waken everyone in the coach. But suppose they did not hear? What if they were not really *asleep*? Tears started in her eyes, magnifying and distorting the print on a page till it became a hazy blur. She shut the magazine with fierce abruptness and looked at the woman.

'I'll buy it,' she said. 'The charm, I mean. I'll buy it, if that's all – just all you want.'

The woman made no response. She smiled apathetically as she turned toward the man.

As Kay watched, the man's face seemed to change form and recede before her like a moon-shaped rock sliding downward under a surface of water. A warm laziness relaxed her. She was dimly conscious of it when the woman took away her purse, and when she gently pulled the raincoat like a shroud above her head.

a little history

Penguin Modern Classics were launched in 1961, and have been shaping the reading habits of generations ever since.

The list began with distinctive grey spines and evocative pictorial covers – a look that, after various incarnations, continues to influence their current design – and with books that are still considered landmark classics today.

Penguin Modern Classics have caused scandal and political change, inspired great films and broken down barriers, whether social, sexual or the boundaries of language itself. They remain the most provocative, groundbreaking, exciting and revolutionary works of the last 100 years (or so).

In 2011, on the fiftieth anniversary of the Modern Classics, we're publishing fifty Mini Modern Classics: the very best short fiction by writers ranging from Beckett to Conrad, Nabokov to Saki, Updike to Wodehouse. Though they don't take long to read, they'll stay with you long after you turn the final page.

MODERN CLASSICS
www.penguinclassics.com